Also by Dosh Archer

Urgency Emergency!

Itsy Bitsy Spider

Big Bad Wolf

Little Elephant's Blocked Trunk

Humpty's Fall

Baaad Sheep

Detective Paw of the Law

The Case of Piggy's Bank

The Case of the Stolen Drumsticks

The Case of the Missing Painting

DETECTIVE PAW
OF THE LAW

The Case of the
Icky Ice Cream

Dosh Archer

Albert Whitman & Company
Chicago, Illinois

To Delphine

Library of Congress Cataloging-in-Publication data
is on file with the publisher.

Text and illustrations copyright © 2020 by Dosh Archer
First published in the United States of America
in 2020 by Albert Whitman & Company
ISBN 978-0-8075-1571-6 (hardcover)
ISBN 978-0-8075-1576-1 (ebook)

Printed in China
10 9 8 7 6 5 4 3 2 1 WKT 24 23 22 21 20 19

Design by Nina D'Amario

For more information about Albert Whitman & Company,
visit our website at www.albertwhitman.com.

Prologue

In the heart of Big City is Big City Police Headquarters.

This is where Detective Paw works with his assistant, Patrol Officer Prickles.

Detective Paw has been a detective for a long time. He has solved many cases. Once he is on the trail of a

criminal, he never gives up, and no
criminal is a match for Detective Paw.

Patrol Office Prickles is always by his
side, ready to assist with his technical

skills, loyalty, and determination.

They solve crime—together. The good residents of Big City can rest easy, knowing the law is in safe hands.

Chapter One

It was a hot summer morning. Detective Paw arrived at his office to find his phone ringing.

It was Patrol Officer Prickles.

"It's Patrol Officer Prickles here. There has been a serious incident at the Dreamy Creamy Ice-Cream Parlor. Can you get here as quickly as possible?"

Detective Paw grabbed his notebook
(for writing down clues), his magnifying
glass (for spotting teeny-tiny clues),
and headed out. The Dreamy Creamy
Ice-Cream Parlor was just around
the corner. On his way Detective Paw
passed the park, where the Gordon's

Cones ice-cream bicycle cart was parked. It was the right kind of day for ice cream, thought Detective Paw.

He arrived at the parlor, where a large model of an ice-cream cone stood outside the entrance. Inside the parlor, Patrol Officer Prickles was waiting.

"This is Floella Flufftail," said Patrol Officer Prickles. "The owner of the parlor." Floella Flufftail was wringing her hands.

One of the customers was coughing and spluttering.

"This is Mr. Abercrombie," said Patrol Officer Prickles. "He has had an unfortunate experience."

"I'll say!" spluttered Mr. Abercrombie.

"Please fetch Mr. Abercrombie a glass of water," said Floella to Sybil Slomo, the waitress.

It took a little while for Sybil to arrive with the water.

"Can't you hurry up?" gasped Mr. Abercrombie.

Eventually Sybil reached the table.

"I am so sorry, Mr. Abercrombie. I have encouraged Sybil to be a little quicker, but speed is not her thing," said Floella.

"Some ice-cream parlor this is!" said Mr. Abercrombie.

"Everyone calm down," said Detective Paw. "Ms. Flufftail, tell me what happened."

"Mr. Abercrombie came in and ordered a vanilla ice-cream sundae with my special, award-winning raspberry syrup," said Floella. "He asked for extra syrup..."

"I wish I hadn't," said Mr. Abercrombie.

"I served the sundae myself, and Mr. Abercrombie took a bite. That's when I found out my raspberry syrup had been swapped for tomato ketchup!" cried Floella. "The bottle was the same one I use for my syrup. But someone emptied it out and put in ketchup! How could this have happened?"

"Ketchup on ice cream! Can you imagine? It tastes HORRIBLE!" said Mr. Abercrombie.

Detective Paw shook his head. "Tell

me what you've got, Prickles," he said. Patrol Officer Prickles consulted his latest police-issue electronic notepad. "I arrived at the scene of the crime at 9:02 a.m. I noted the following things:

1. There is raspberry syrup in the sink.

2. In the backyard, there are some red drops in a trail leading out the back gate, through the alleyway, to the main road.

3. There is NO sign of a break-in.

4. The potted plant in the backyard has been knocked over."

Detective Paw nodded. "Now I must ask that no one leaves the parlor, and no one comes in either," he said.

Patrol Officer Prickles put special-issue police tape across the door, to make sure no one else

could get into the scene of the crime.

Everyone looked at Detective Paw. There was Mr. Abercrombie, who was still coughing and spluttering. There were Blaze, Jake, and Spike, the three

members of the Rowdy Riders Gang. They had parked their BMX bikes outside. There were Floella Flufftail and the waitress, Sybil Slomo.

Detective Paw popped a peppermint into his mouth to help him think. "I will get to the bottom of this," he said.

Chapter Two

"I need to speak with each of you," said Detective Paw. "Ms. Flufftail, I will start with you."

They went into the kitchen. Detective Paw noticed a freezer with a glass door. Inside was a large ice-cream cake with "Wilma" written in gold letters on top.

"I have a birthday party booked for

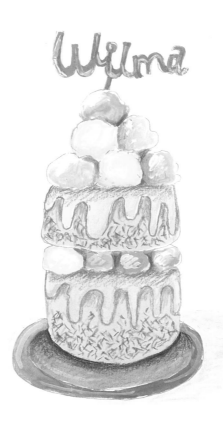

one o'clock today for Wilma Sparkles,"
said Floella. "I made this cake for her.
It's got raspberry, strawberry, and
vanilla ice cream with butterscotch
crunch topping. She will be seven! Solve
this crime, Detective Paw, so the party
can go ahead!"

"Tell me how you started your day," said Detective Paw.

"After I opened the parlor, I went out front to water my window boxes. Then Sybil arrived late. She is quite slow, as you have seen." Floella said. "Then I got my special raspberry syrup from the kitchen and waited for the customers to arrive. You know what happened after that!"

Detective Paw made some notes. "Tell me about the other customers here," he said.

"The Rowdy Riders come in a lot," said Floella. "They are crazy about chocolate ice cream. But sometimes they are rowdy. Yesterday I had to tell them to be quiet so the other customers could enjoy their ice cream in peace."

"Thank you, Ms. Flufftail," said Detective Paw. "That will be all for now."

Detective Paw called in the Rowdy Riders.

"I hear you have been making too much noise," said Detective Paw.

"Sorry," said Blaze.

"What were you doing last night and this morning?" Detective Paw asked them.

"We all had a sleepover last night," said Jake.

"And this morning we practiced nose wheelies in the park before coming here," said Spike.

"Thank you," said Detective Paw. "You may go back to the parlor."

Next was Sybil Slomo, the waitress. Detective Paw and Patrol Officer Prickles waited as she made her way into the kitchen. She explained that she had missed the bus that morning.

"That's why I was late," she said. "But I like working here! Ms. Flufftail gave

me a pep talk about getting ice cream to the table before it melts. I like a challenge. I'm getting better!"

Sybil smiled.

"Thank you," said Detective Paw. "That will be all for now."

"What else have you got to show me, Prickles?" said Detective Paw. Prickles led him into the backyard.

Detective Paw used his magnifying glass to study the trail of red spots. "These are still wet," said Detective Paw, "so that means they were spilled this morning." He looked

closer. "I think they are tomato ketchup. Can you test them, Prickles?"

Patrol Officer Prickles used his special police-issue substance-detector kit to test the drops. The results were ketchup affirmative.

They followed the drops through the backyard, out the gate, through the alleyway at the side of the shop, then along the pavement for about a block, where the drops stopped.

"Hmmm," said Detective Paw, "interesting." He made more notes.

Prickles took a photograph of the drops for investigative purposes.

"I wonder why the drops stop so suddenly," said Detective Paw. "Maybe someone was carrying a dripping ketchup bottle, and got in a vehicle of some kind, right here, and left."

Chapter Three

Detective Paw looked over to the park. He noticed the Gordon's Cones bicycle cart had a long line of customers.

"Gordon's cart was not so busy when I passed it this morning," said Detective Paw. "Let's take a look."

At the ice-cream cart, Detective Paw held up his badge and said, "Excuse me,

sir, could I have a word with you?"

Gordon came around from behind the cart, limping.

"Did you see anything unusual this morning outside the Dreamy Creamy Ice-Cream Parlor?" said Detective Paw.

"NO," said Gordon. "And I stubbed my toe this morning, so I don't feel like talking."

"How did you stub your toe?" said
Detective Paw.

"I forget," said Gordon. He looked
away.

"That will be all for now," said
Detective Paw, stroking his mustache.

Gordon limped back behind the cart.

"Let's go for a short walk," said Detective Paw to Patrol Officer Prickles. "I need to think."

They strolled down the street.

"Hmmm," said Detective Paw. "The suspects I have interviewed so far all say they were somewhere else this morning when the crime was committed, and I think they are telling the truth. So who could the culprit be?"

Detective Paw scratched his head. "This is a two-peppermint problem." He popped another peppermint into his mouth to help him think extra hard.

After he had thought extra hard, he said, "I have a feeling Gordon is not telling us something. Did you notice the way he couldn't look me in the eye? I want to have another chat with him."

Chapter Four

As they arrived back at Gordon's Cones, Detective Paw spotted an empty bottle of tomato ketchup in the trash can behind the cart.

"Hmmm," said Detective Paw. He made some notes, and Prickles took a photograph of the trash can for investigative purposes.

Detective Paw stepped to the front of

the line. "Gordon," he said, "I couldn't help but notice an empty bottle of ketchup in your trash can."

"So what?" said Gordon.

"Well," said Detective Paw. "Someone swapped Ms. Flufftail's award-winning raspberry syrup for ketchup this morning, and she can't open her ice-cream parlor until we find out who did it. And if she can't open the parlor, the birthday party will have to be cancelled..."

"Well that's too bad for Wilma," said Gordon, "but that has nothing to do with me."

"Gordon," said Detective Paw. "You are under arrest for swapping the raspberry syrup for tomato ketchup with bad intentions. Take him into custody, Prickles."

But before Patrol Officer Prickles could get the handcuffs on, Gordon jumped onto the bike and pedaled off as fast as he could.

"Quick, Prickles," shouted Detective Paw. "Let's take your car!"

They raced to Patrol Officer Prickles's Arrester police car, which was outside Police Headquarters, jumped in, and sped off.

"Don't lose him, Prickles," shouted Detective Paw as they saw Gordon turn a corner on the road ahead.

Patrol Office Prickles took the corner at high speed, controlling the wheel with his excellent steering reflexes and the use of his police-issue tough-grip driving gloves.

Soon they were just inches away from Gordon. The hot sun was superbright, glinting off the windshield into Patrol Officer Prickles's eyes. He wasn't bothered, because he was wearing his police-issue nonreflective polarized sunglasses with side visors.

Blinded by the sun,

Gordon squinted his eyes as he lost control of the bicycle cart.

Scrreeeeechhhh!

CRAASHHH!

Patrol Office Prickles made a reverse spin, pulling up the Arrester car safely to the curb. He jumped out and handcuffed Gordon, who luckily wasn't hurt, just very sticky.

Patrol Officer Prickles put him in the car once Detective Paw had put down some paper towels to protect the seats.

"It's better if you tell the truth," said Detective Paw to Gordon.

"Floella Flufftail's ice cream was better than mine, and I don't have a special raspberry syrup, so her parlor got all the customers," said Gordon. "I wanted to stop people from going there so they would come to me."

"I parked my bicycle cart a block away this morning," he continued, "and when Floella Flufftail went out to water her petunias, she left the door open. I sneaked along the wall, hid behind the big ice cream, and slipped through the parlor into the kitchen, where I emptied the syrup bottle and squeezed the ketchup bottle to fill it back up. I ran out the back door, but I stubbed my toe on the stupid plant pot."

"The ketchup drops were a clue," said Detective Paw.

On the way back to Police Headquarters, the police car stopped outside The Dreamy Creamy Ice-Cream Parlor. It was almost one o'clock, and Wilma Sparkles and her family were waiting outside with fingers crossed.

Detective Paw stepped out to speak to everyone.

"I am pleased to say we have arrested the person who spoiled the ice cream, so you will be able to have the party after all!"

A cheer went up.

Back at Police Headquarters, Detective Paw said to Gordon, "What you did was wrong. It affected Mr. Abercrombie, and if we hadn't caught you, people might have heard about it and thought Ms. Flufftail was careless. And you nearly ruined the party of Wilma Sparkles, who is seven today."

"How did you know it was me?" asked Gordon.

"That was easy," said Detective Paw. "You knew the name of the person having the birthday party. You couldn't have known that unless you'd seen the birthday cake. And then the fact that you'd seen the cake meant you'd been in the kitchen."

Detective Paw explained to Gordon that it's wrong to spoil someone else's hard work just because you aren't doing very well. It is much better to improve yourself and work together with people.

Gordon was sent to a jail cell to wait for Judge Joan to decide his punishment.